Steel Drums

Steel Drums

and other Stories and Poems from around the World

Ann Marie Linden

illustrated by Valerie McBride

BBC BOOKS

Published by BBC Books,
a division of BBC Enterprises Limited
Woodlands, 80 Wood Lane, London W12 0TT
First published 1992
© Ann Marie Linden 1992
The moral right of the author has been asserted

ISBN 0 563 36375 4

Set in 14/17pt Plantin Roman
by Goodfellow & Egan, Cambridge
Printed and bound in Great Britain by
Clays Ltd, St Ives plc
Cover printed by Clays Ltd, St Ives plc

Contents

For Ron Tills, with thanks.
Sorry about the ironing.

About the author

Ann Marie Linden was born in Barbados in the Caribbean. She grew up with her brother in the loving care of her grandmother to whom her first picture book, *One Smiling Grandma* (Heinemann) is attributed.

She now lives in London and works in Westminster City Libraries as an organiser of storytelling activities and reading schemes for children. She contributes to BBC TV's *Playdays* series and some of the stories and poems in this collection have appeared in the *Playdays* magazine.

Ann Marie travels regularly through India and other countries – "adding spice and colour to my writing and to my life". *Steel Drums and other Stories and Poems from around the World* is her first anthology.

APPLE GRUMBLE

The day I made an apple crumble,
Everyone mumbled, rumbled and
   grumbled.
It wasn't my fault,
That I added salt,
The jar on the table
Should have been labelled.
Yes, the crumble is tough,
But there wasn't enough
Butter or lard
And the marg was hard.
But it doesn't taste bad
If you'd only add
A dollop of cream,
Then *mmm* . . . it's a dream!

SUMMER

I lie on my back
And look at the sky,
As clouds like elephants
Roll on by.
The sun is warm
A cool wind blows,
I can smell the scent
Of the sweet red rose.
The bumble bees hum,
A bird shrilly sings,
The crickets chirrup
As summer brings
Strawberries and raspberries
And blackberries too,
Poppies and buttercups
And cornflower blue.

ONE PINK SARI

One pink sari for a pretty girl,

Two dancing women all in a whirl,

Three charmed cobras rising from
a basket,

Four fat rubies, in the Rajah's casket,

Five water carriers straight and tall,

Six wicked vultures sitting on the wall,

Seven fierce tigers hiding in the grass,

Eight elephants rolling in a warm
mud bath,

Nine green parrots in the coconut tree,

Ten twinkling stars, a-twinkling at me!

STEEL DRUMS

John James was born in England, but his mummy and daddy were born on an island in the Caribbean called Barbados. John loved listening to their stories about life on the island. He especially enjoyed hearing stories about the steel bands that played on the beaches in the warm sunshine. John had never heard a steel band play, but how he wished that he could!

On Saturday morning, John went shopping with his mummy and daddy at the big market in town. John loved the busy market place because there were so many different things to see.

There were Nigerian women who wore short, patterned blouses and long, patterned skirts. Around their waists they had wrapped a long wide piece of cloth called an oja. Some of the women carried their babies on their backs in the oja. They also wore colourful turbans on their heads. John thought they looked magnificent.

Next, he saw some Asian women wearing bright saris and shalwar-kameeze. They were chatting noisily outside the grocer's shop which sold Indian foods and spices. John liked the smell of this shop best of all.

Next door to the grocer's was the music shop, which sold records and cassettes. The owner of the shop was Mr Baptiste. He wore his hair in long plaits called dreadlocks.

"Hello, John Jones," called out Mr Baptiste as John passed by.

"Hello, Mr Baptiste," replied John Jones. He felt very pleased that Mr Baptiste had remembered him.

John's mummy stopped at Mr

Devaux's market stall to buy special fruit and vegetables that had been grown in a hot country, just like the one where John's parents came from. John liked the way Mr Devaux called out in a loud booming voice: "Come buy my fresh breadfruit! Come buy my sweet paw-paw!"

Mummy chose fine juicy ripe mangoes, a yellow pineapple, three hairy coconuts, six rough yams and some sweet potatoes. Mr Devaux cut the coconut into squares and gave John a piece. John thanked him, then helped Daddy to pack everything away neatly in the shopping bag.

Next they went to Miss Wilma's fabric shop. Mummy liked to sew her own clothes, so she wanted to buy some pretty material. While she was deciding

whether to buy the red dotted or the red stripy material, they heard a loud cheering noise coming from the other side of the market place.

"Look," said Daddy, "it's a steel band. It looks as if they are about to start playing."

"Let's go and watch," said Mummy. Daddy carried the heavy shopping while Mummy held tight to John's hand and they hurried across the busy market square.

John stood in front of the fat shiny drums. He felt very excited. He couldn't wait to hear them play.

The steel band were outside a cafe that had just opened. It was called *The Red Hot Pepper*. The steel band were going to play to welcome the new customers. The members of the band wore red T-shirts with the words RED HOT PEPPER printed across them in big, black letters. The girls had shiny red and black beads in their plaited hair.

There were tables and chairs outside the cafe, so Mummy, Daddy and John Jones sat down to wait for the music to start. A waiter came over and Daddy ordered three mango milkshakes and a large plate of plantain chips. "*One, two three!*" shouted the band leader. The band started to play a light and bouncy tune that made everyone feel happy. Some people started to dance and sing, and a baby in a pram gurgled happily and clapped her hands.

John loved the sounds the steel drums made. "I bet it's as good as the steel band Mummy and Daddy heard on the beach," he thought, as he sipped his drink and tapped his feet to the steel drums' beat!

ELEPHANT

The elephant is an
enormous beast.
It likes to eat a
magnificent feast
Of grasses
and leaves
and fruits
and flowers,
It uses its trunk for cooling showers.
It has ivory tusks and wrinkly skin
And makes such a din
when it's
trumpeting!

SOUNDS OF THE SEA

Sometimes the sea sighs
When it breathes easy.
Sometimes when angry
It rises up
With a deafening roar
And smashes against
The sandy floor.
Sometimes the evening breeze
Makes it smoothly flow
To sleepily slap
On the silvery shore.

SAND AND FOAM

Green is the colour of sweet round peas
And the whispering leaves on the big
    palm trees.

Yellow is the colour of pineapples sweet
And ripe bananas ready to eat.

Blue is the colour of sea and sky
And flying fish flashing by.

Red is the colour of monkey tails merry
Bottle brush flowers and the sour cherry.

Orange is the colour of the setting sun
And the light in the sky when the day is
    done.

Black is the colour of the night-time bat
And the howling, prowling midnight
    cat.

White is the colour of sand and foam
And the new moon's light which guides
    us home.

THE WANDERING PENNY

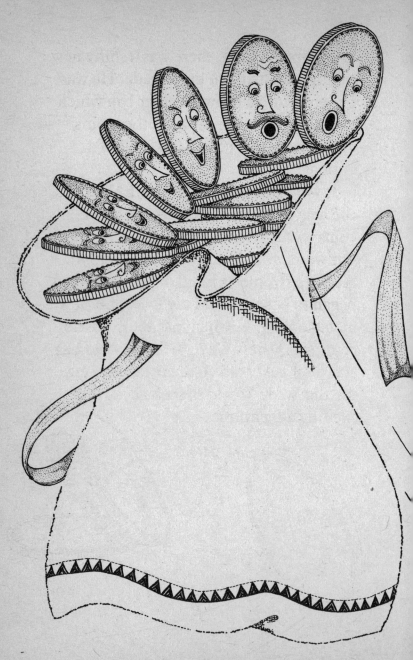

Once upon a time, there was a shiny new penny who had just been made. He was dropped into a brown leather bag which was filled to the brim with other coins and placed high on the top shelf of a cupboard in the bank.

It was dark and gloomy in the bag and the new penny noticed that the other coins were not as shiny bright as he was, but were rather dull and worn-looking. He felt extremely proud of his gleam and began to boast about how lovely his new metal looked. He then told the coins he could not wait to leave the musty old bag and their rusty old company and go into the Big Wide World to seek all sorts of exciting adventures.

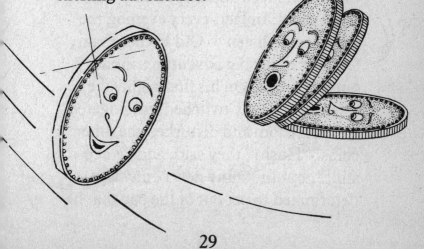

The other pennies were shocked by the new penny's rudeness and bad manners. One old penny, who was particularly rusty and worn and was called Old Father Penny, gruffly said, "Young brother, do not be in a hurry to leave us, for the day will come when you will wish to return."

"Never," piped the new penny.

"Ah," said Father Penny knowingly, "So you say, but we have seen the Big Wide World and know it to be not all happiness and good adventures there."

The shiny new penny sulked and thought Old Father Penny was boring, but did not dare say so as the old penny was much loved and respected by the other coins. In fact, every evening the coins would listen to Old Father Penny tell tales of his big adventures in the outside world. On his first night, the shiny new penny twitched and fidgeted with boredom and disturbed the other coins. "Hush!" they said, and "Keep still!", but the shiny new penny was so determined to get out of the bag that he rubbed his head against the soft leather in order to make a hole through which he could escape.

One evening, many moons later, when Old Father Penny had told his tales and the coins were settling down for the night, there came a knocking and a banging and a great crashing noise, as if the sky was falling down upon them.

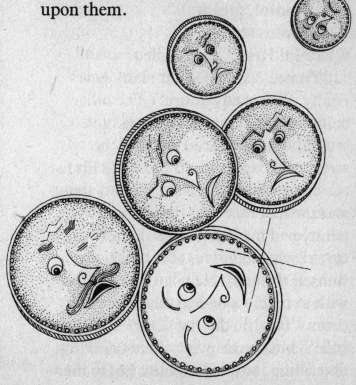

Suddenly the cupboard doors were wrenched wide open and the old leather bag was snatched from the top shelf.

"Oh lordy me," trembled an old lady coin. "What is happening?"

"I fear," said Old Father Penny solemnly, "it is a bank robbery and we are being stolen."

"Oh! Oh!" cried some of the coins.

"Dreadful, dreadful!"

"Heavens above!"

"Help! Help!" they wailed.

"Yippee!" shrieked the shiny new penny, "a real adventure!" The other coins looked at him disapprovingly.

As the robber raced through the street, the bag clutched tightly in his fist, the coins were dashed and jiggled about and the tiny hole that the shiny new penny had made now split open a very tiny crack and he was able to squeeze himself through. He fell to the ground with a clink. As he had fallen face downwards, he did not see the midnight blue sky with the pretty stars twinkling above him, but nevertheless he lay there

happy and free until the morning light brought the children out of their homes and along the path where he lay.

A crowd of children passed him by, laughing and chattering on their way to school. He twitched with excitement and, as he did so, the sun caught the gleam of his new metal and little Lucy who came skipping by noticed the bright penny and picked him up. She put him in her pocket.

Inside Lucy's pocket was a half-eaten toffee bar which was warm, sticky and smelt of treacle.

"'allo, mate," shouted the toffee cheerfully. "I'm Mr Chewitt. Who might you be, then?"

The shiny new penny wrinkled his nose and turned his back to the toffee.

"Coo, I've met some toffee-noses in my life, but you beat the lot. You can't have airs and graces in pockets, mate, you never know what's gonna fall on you."

"Oh? Like what?" asked the shiny new penny nervously.

"Ooh, fluff and stuff," replied the toffee airily and promptly curled up and went to sleep. He began to snore. It was very loud, like a train rumbling over a bridge. It even had a whistle. The shiny new penny felt sticky and cross. This, he decided, was not a good adventure.

By and by the toffee woke up and s-t-r-e-t-c-h-e-d. "Time for lunch," he said as Lucy pulled out the half-eaten toffee bar and finished it up.

"Peace at last," sighed the penny but, before he could enjoy it, he was snatched from the pocket and slapped on to a smooth wooden counter.

Lucy was in the sweetshop and was buying another Mr Chewitt bar. Mr Mint, the sweetshop owner, picked the penny up carefully and looked at it crossly. It was covered in stickiness. He was about to drop it in the till when in charged Lucy's brother, James. James had curly brown hair, freckles and an impish look about him. He bought a bag of crisps and Mr Mint gave Lucy's sticky

penny to James as change.

James dropped the penny into his pocket – what a pocket! There was something lumpy and green in it. "RIVETT!" croaked the lumpy, green thing. Frightened, the shiny new penny rolled behind something red and blobby which wobbled with laughter, but smelt quite nice. The penny peered around the red, blobby, wobbly thing and noticed something else. It was hard, small and white, half wrapped in cottonwool and it shone in the gloomy darkness of the pocket.

"Don't you know it's rude to stare?" it told the penny.

"Sorry," said the penny, "I was only wondering what you are."

"I'm Mr Molar, a tooth," it said. "I bite, crunch and tear things but sadly I can no longer perform these feats. As you see, I have fallen out of Master James's mouth. It was one of those Mr Chewitt bars what did it. Too blooming chewy, if you ask me." And he sniffed sadly.

The penny was speechless. He had never met, heard of nor seen such peculiar things. He wished and wished to be away from this madness and, as if in answer to his wish, he slipped through a hole in James's pocket and fell on to the hard pavement. He rolled a little way, swayed, then fell face downwards into the gutter.

There he lay for many months. He did not see the summer, but only felt the heat of the hot sun burning down on his back. He did not see the blustery autumn, but the rainwater trickled down the gutter and washed the dead leaves and bits of conkers over him. Neither did he see the icy winter, but the cold

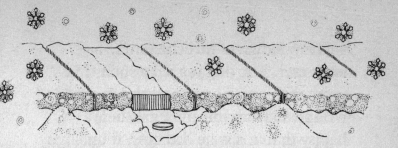

crisp snow weighed heavily on him and he was deeply sad. His face was streaked rusty by fat tears that rolled silently down his flat, round face and all the time he lay there the cars, lorries and trucks rushed past him. Above him, on the hard pavement, people hurried by and no one noticed him.

Early one spring morning, a little boy came hurrying along. His laces were untied but he was in too much of a hurry to stop and tie them. So it was not long before they tripped him up and sent him sprawling across the pavement. As he picked himself up, his sharp eyes noticed the penny in the gutter.

"See a penny and pick it up, all the day you'll have good luck," he sang, and that is exactly what he did. He picked it up, took it home and dropped it into a blue glass pig that stood solidly on the

window ledge in the little boy's
bedroom. The pig was fed to bursting
point with silver coins and the penny
wriggled his way in amongst them,
happy that at last he had been found.

"Oi!" shouted a silver coin nastily,

"Watch where you're going!"

"So sorry," said the penny humbly.
"Let me introduce myself, I'm a shiny
new penny and I . . ." He did not finish
what he was saying because his voice was
lost in the roars of laughter that were
coming from the other coins.

"Ha, ha, ha! Ho, ho, hee!" they
roared. "What a joker! What a clown!"

The penny felt angry, for he did not

know what was making them laugh.

The penny looked down at himself and was shocked to see that he had become very rusty and worn. He blushed with shame and said no more to the silver coins. After a little while, their laughing and teasing stopped and they soon forgot about him and went back to gossiping and arguing amongst themselves.

It was horrible being there and he wished for his old home. He longed for the warmth of the old leather bag, its musty smell and the kindness of the rusty coins. He especially missed Old Father Penny's stories as the night-time came. He looked up through the chink in the top of the pig and to his delight he could see the stars in the midnight sky. He had never seen the stars before and he saw that they were more beautiful and more shiny than anything he had ever seen. They seemed to be twinkling at him. He found this very comforting and soon fell fast asleep.

The next day, the little boy came into

the room and emptied all the coins from
the blue glass pig on to his bed. He then
scooped them into a bag and went out of
the house.

The coins all wondered what they
were to be spent on. "Probably
hundreds of Mr Chewitt toffee bars,"

said one particularly miserable silver coin. "I've bought hundreds of those nasty sticky things."

"I bet it's a bicycle," said another.

"No, no, no! It's a computer," some said.

But it was none of these things, for the boy went into the bank at the far end of the street and proudly emptied the bag of coins on to the counter. The child was saving up for a train set. Mr Tills, the bank manager, put all the silver coins (still arguing and fighting) into one bag and dropped the rusty penny into an old familiar musty leather bag and placed it on the top shelf of the cupboard in the bank.

The penny fell into a corner of the bag, just where a new brown patch had been sewn. It was the very place where the penny, when he was shiny and new, had rubbed and rubbed to make a hole. He could hardly believe his luck. The bank robber had been caught red-handed and the bag of coins returned to the bank.

He looked around shyly and noticed Old Father Penny looking at him with a kindly smile on his worn, flat face. "Well, brother, it's good to see you back," he said.

The penny's heart swelled with joy. He felt very, very happy. "It's good to be back," said the little coin quietly, as happy tears flowed down his face. "I have missed you all."

And they made room for him as he joined them to listen to Old Father Penny's tale of how, one night, a robber came and stole them all.

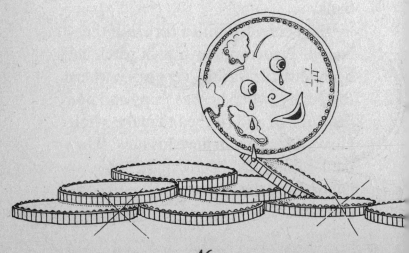

COCONUT GROOVE

At the coconut groove
See everybody move,
They boogie together
Despite the weather.
It's raining, it's blowing
But the rhythm is flowing,
As the frog from France
With agouti break-dance.
Frisky mongoose
Lets it all hang loose,
While the slippery snake
Does the S-bend shake.
With the monkeys on drums
The humming birds hum.
The music's so good
Down here in the woods.
Juicy Miss Mango
Does a daring tango,
With Mr Jackfruit
In his fine green suit.
The potatoes look sweet
As they bop to the beat,
As everybody swings
And does their thing
Down at the coconut groove.

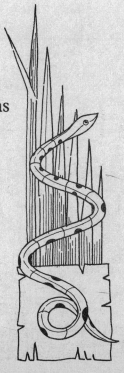

CLOTHES

I like the red dotted shirt

And the blue stripy skirt.

And the green
satin dress,

Is the one I wear for best,

But the warm woolly jumper,
Makes me look a lot plumper

Than I really am!

WISHES

I'd like to hug
The lions in the zoo

And speckle my house
Green, yellow and blue.

And swim in a pool
Of orange that's fizzy

52

And spin on the roundabouts
Without getting

And own a forever-chocolate cake,
(That doesn't give you a stomach ache),

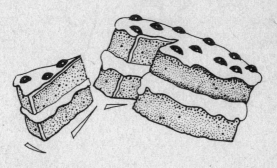

And a bed that keeps you wide-awake –
Until Father Christmas comes.

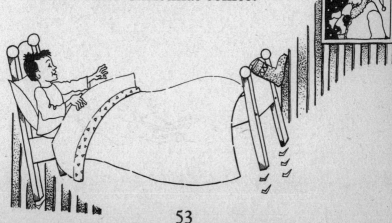

A DOG DAY

There is a library which has a kind, friendly librarian called Miss Tumilty. Most of the children find that name very hard to say, so they call her Miss Tumtee.

Miss Tumtee has silver hair, round glasses, and a cotton dress with a bow at the neck.

Many children visit Miss Tumtee's library. They come from different countries and speak different languages. Miss Tumtee always makes sure that the library has books about everyone's country, so that each person feels important.

Every afternoon there is storytime, and if the story is about the country that you come from, you can sit in the special story chair.

Early one morning, there was a banging on the library door.

"Miss Tumtee! Help!"

Miss Tumtee quickly opened the door. Robert and Mimi were there.

They looked very scared.

"Whatever is the matter?" asked Miss Tumtee. She led them inside and sat them down. "Has somebody hurt you?"

Robert shook his head.

Mimi just said, "Monster," and two fat tears slid down her cheeks.

Robert and Mimi's big sisters, Jane and Nasreen, came in.

"What has happened to the children?" asked Miss Tumtee.

"We were on our way to the library and they saw a dog," said Jane.

"They were frightened and they ran all the way here," continued Nasreen. "The dog followed them – all the way, too!"

There was a whining and scratching noise. Robert and Mimi clung to each other. Miss Tumtee opened the door and there stood a shaggy little dog with a wagging tail.

"It only wants to play," she said.

"We know where it lives," said Jane. "We'll take it home."

While they were gone, Miss Tumtee

showed Robert and Mimi a picture book about different kinds of dogs. She explained that some dogs were friendly, loving pets, but should only be patted with the owners' permission. And she said that other dogs were big bullies, and they *definitely* ought to be left alone.

Miss Tumtee reminded them that Sarah, who was blind, would be coming that morning to tell them all about her guide dog, Rosie.

So Robert and Mimi settled down with a book each, and waited for her to arrive.

The library soon filled with children and parents, and at ten o'clock exactly, Sarah appeared with Rosie.

She told them that Rosie was very well-behaved and loved children, so they could all stroke her. Rosie thumped her tail on the carpet and looked pleased. Sarah explained that Rosie was specially trained to help blind people, and that Rosie could take her across the road safely and stop her from bumping into lamp posts.

Then Sarah took off Rosie's harness and let Robert put it on. Mimi pretended to be blind and Robert guided her round the library. It was very exciting. Then the children asked Sarah lots of questions.

A photographer took pictures, and the next day they were printed on the front page of the local paper. And guess what? There in the picture, with their arms around Rosie's neck, were Robert and Mimi!

AUTUMN

Raincoats, wellingtons
Tramping through leaves
Throwing sticks at conker trees.
Strong winds blowing,
Bonfires burning,
This is how the autumn feels.
Raindrops falling,
Swallows are calling,
Time to fly to warmer lands.
With mittens on hands
And scarves wrapped tight,
Children are celebrating
Firework Night.

AN INDIAN DAY

A girl in a sari with a gold ring through
    her nose
Wears pretty sequinned slippers with
    curled up toes.
Her spicy lentils bubble on an iron
    stove
As black buffaloes bask in the mango
    grove
And cows chewing cud calmly stand and
    stare
As camels carry caskets of coral rare,
Cargoes of precious stones, spices and
    carpets
Silks and pistachios for Delhi's old
    markets.
A corner in the courtyard, a cobra
    uncoils,
A tailor stitching waistcoats on a charpoy
    toils.
Musicians softly sing as they tap out the
    beat,
It's time for tiffin in the midday heat.
At the bustling bazaar it's noisy and
    busy

As buyers barter for sandalwood and
 bhindi,
Incense and bangles and beautiful
 brassware,
While above on the balconies bright
 bedrolls air.
Elephants and bicycles and bier pass by
And a buzzard watches all with a beady
 eye.

CHRISTMAS

Outside, softly and silently
Falls the snow
And gently settles
On the earth below.
From a warm nest
On a snow-laden tree,
A robin red-breast
Chirrups merrily.

Inside the house
The tree is lit
And the Christmas presents
Are piled under it.
In the kitchen
The child helps bake
Spicy mince pies
And a Christmas cake.
But now the hour
Is getting late,
The grandfather clock
Is striking eight.
It's time for bed
My sleepy head
It will soon be Christmas morning.

IN A FARAWAY CORNER

In a faraway corner
of my mind,
There lives a King
Who is good and kind.
He is tall and noble
Strong and true,
And shimmers with light
All shades of blue.
He never commands
But I always feel
The correct thing to do
Is bow and kneel.
Then by his feet
A cushion placed,
I take my seat
And watch his face.
A face that's Ancient,
Brave and Wise,
With a snow-white beard
And twinkling brown eyes.
He gives me a nod,
He gives me a wink,
He smiles and asks me
Whether I think

My tasks for the night
Should be hard
Or light.
You choose, says I,
Then I'll know
It is right.

COUNTING

Ten tall vicars sitting down to dine
Blow wind, blow, and that leaves nine.

Nine boys and girls swinging on a gate,
Blow wind, blow, and that leaves eight.

Eight twinkly stars, shining in the
 heavens,
Blow wind, blow, and that leaves seven.

Seven fat gardeners picking up sticks,
Blow wind, blow, and that leaves six.

Six busy bees buzzing by the hive,
Blow wind, blow, and that leaves five.

Five spinning spiders above my door,
Blow wind, blow, and that leaves four.

Four shivering leaves on the big oak
    tree,
Blow wind, blow, and that leaves three.

Three white storks flying over the zoo,
Blow wind, blow, and that leaves two.

Two yellow shirts drying in the sun,
Blow wind, blow, and that leaves one.

One little girl with an iced currant bun,
Blow wind, blow, and that leaves none.

HURRICANE

The hurricane has come
The winds fiercely blow
Tearing off roof tops
Bending palm trees low.
Rattling on windows
Banging on doors
Screaming down keyholes
Then howling some more.
It swirls and it whirls
Tin cans in the air
Then hurtles on by
Without any care.

INTO THE NIGHT

Stepping on out into the night

Moon and stars both shining bright

Swinging on up on the Milky Way,

To the heavenly music we gently sway.

Up and up, pierce through the Light,

Behold, an emerald palace in sight.

On and on, we dance to the beat

With golden wings upon our feet,

And enter through a ruby door

To tread upon a marble floor.

And before us on a chair is sat . . .

AAHHH! I'm suddenly awakened by
my cat!

Also published by BBC Books

I'D LIKE TO BE A TEABAG AND OTHER POEMS

I'd Like to be a Teabag brings together a selection of poems edited by Susan Roberts and featured in BBC Radio 5's exciting poetry programme for older children, *Talking Poetry*. The collection's scope is wide, taking in the work of past masters such as Lewis Carroll and up-to-date favourites including Michael Rosen, Brian Patten, Roger McGough, and Peter Dixon, whose teabag it was in the first place. The anthology includes poems on: food, trains and stations, sleep and dreams, the sea, music, fantasy, conflict – and much more.

And for younger children

PLAYDAYS

Four fun-filled activity books by Ann Reay,
featuring the characters from BBC TV's *Playdays*
programme:

COLOURS AND SHAPES
LETTERS AND WORDS
NUMBERS
OUT AND ABOUT

PLAYDAYS

Ann Reay has also compiled four lively picture story books featuring the characters from BBC TV's highly popular *Playdays* programme:

BE HAPPY! AND OTHER RHYMES
AND GAMES
HUMBERT THE HUNGRY HARE
JOLLY JUICE JAM FACTORY
UNSCARY SPIDER